The [

of

Robin's Toys

Ken and Angie Lake

Gavin the Gorilla and Snuffles

Published by Sweet Cherry Publishing Limited
53 St. Stephens Road,
Leicester, LE2 1GH
United Kingdom

First Published in the UK in 2013

ISBN: 978-1-78226-024-0
Text: © Ken and Angie Lake 2013
Illustrations: (c) Vishnu Madhav,
Creative Books

Title: Gavin the Gorrilla and Snuffles - The Diaries of Robin's Toys

Printed and Bound By Nutech Print Services, India

_____

Every Toy Has a Story to Tell

Have you ever seen an old toy, perhaps in a cupboard, or in the attic or loft? Have you ever seen how sad they look at car boot sales, unwanted and unloved? Well, look at them closely, because every toy has a story to tell, and the older, the more decrepit, the more scruffy, the more tatty the toy is, the more interesting its story could be. Here are just a few of those toys and their stories.

20th May, 09.25

It was one of those Sunday mornings, you know the sort - high bubbly clouds, dark grey at the bottom and brighter at the top where the sun is bouncing off the fluffy bits.

Robin's mind wandered as he drew the skyline he could see from the window. He thought about his last week at school and a little boy who'd been moved into his class. Mark Philips was extremely shy and kept himself to himself, so it was hardly surprising that Robin had seen him being picked on all week by the other children. He was very small and very thin, and tried very hard to avoid everybody.

Robin couldn't stand to see other children being picked on, and he'd invited Mark over to play on Friday afternoon.

Robin often saw Mark playing with a cricket ball and thought this would be a good way to start a conversation.

"Hello, my name's Robin. I'm in your class," he said. "I've noticed that you always carry a cricket ball around with you."

"Yes," answered Mark, "it's my lucky charm. I love cricket."

"Really?" said Robin. "Me too! Would you like to come over to my house and play later?"

So Mark had come round to play on Friday, but Robin was not prepared for the surprise he got. He gently bowled the cricket ball to Mark so as not to hurt him if it hit him, but Mark hit the ball with an almighty wallop, and it was off into space. It took them ages to find it, but it turned up in the nearby playing fields.

Robin had always thought he was quite good at cricket, but Mark was playing at a much higher level. He would never have thought that someone who got such a hard time from his classmates could actually be so talented.

Robin's mind switched back to Sunday morning as he watched poor old Mrs Bagshaw feeding the birds.

At first a flock of starlings was fighting over the bread; then a big white seagull swooped down and snatched a whole slice.

It soared up into the sky, chased by some others. Robin watched through the window as the seagull gang flew in front of the big fluffy clouds and squabbled over the bread.

They were chasing and diving, chasing and diving, trying to steal the bread. Suddenly, the big seagull dropped the slice of bread and it floated gently down from the sky.

By this time poor old Mrs Bagshaw was wandering down the street pulling her shopping trolley.

It was one of those basket things with two wheels, and it had a walking stick handle.

Robin could not believe what happened next.

The slice of bread floated down and landed inside Mrs Bagshaw's shopping trolley, but she didn't even notice. Robin laughed and laughed and laughed.

"What are you laughing at?" his mum asked.

Robin told her exactly what had happened and she laughed too.

"Well, poor old Mrs Bagshaw has a slice of her bread back; it's a pity that it has been chewed by the seagulls."

Robin was still laughing when he saw his grandad's little red car turn into the street.

Beep, beep, beep, beep!

"Come on, Robin, it's Sunday morning. Let's go to the car boot sale."

By the time they arrived, the clouds had blown away, the sun was shining and everybody was smiling.

"Okay, Robin, here is 50 pence to spend. What toy do you think you will buy today?"

"Oh, I'm not sure, Grandad. It has to be an interesting toy, with a fascinating past and a good story to tell."

"Alright then, let's go and look at Norman's Nick-Nacks stall. He has lots of unusual toys. I have no idea where he gets them from."

Norman had lots of normal nick-nacks that week, but he also had some more unusual stuff in an old cardboard box under his stall.

"Err, excuse me, Mr Nick-Nacks, may I have a look in the cardboard box?" Robin asked.

"Yes, of course you can, son. Everything here is for sale. Help yourself."

Robin had a good rummage around, and right at the bottom, under some paperback books, he spotted a black furry gorilla.

"Grandad, Grandad, look!

This is the nicest gorilla
I have ever seen at the car
boot sale. Do you think he has
had an interesting life?"

Grandad had the magical
power to speak to toys, so he
said, "Let me have a talk with
him first to see if he has lots
to tell us."

Grandad cast a secret spell and seemed to go into a trance.

"Ah yes, Robin, he certainly has a story to tell, but he may not want to leave his friend. You had better ask the stall owner about that."

"Err, excuse me, Mr Nick-Nacks, but how much is this toy gorilla?"

"Well, son, you see there is a bit of a problem with him, and that's why he was hidden in the bottom of the box."

"Oh? He looks alright to me."

"Yes, well, he does look alright, but he is very friendly with a little dog, and they go everywhere together. I can't separate them, so I have to sell them both."

"Where is the little dog, then?"

"Oh, he is at the back of the box. His name is Snuffles. But do be careful, he may bite."

They both laughed.

"So, Mr Nick-Nacks, how much do you want for them both?"

"Well, I really wanted 50 pence for each."

"Oh, I am sorry, I only have 50 pence. I shall have to choose something else."

"Oh alright. If you promise to keep them together, you can have them both for 50 pence."

"Oh, thank you so much."

"Shall I put them in a bag for you?"

"Yes please, Mr Nick-Nacks. By the way, what's the gorilla's name?"

"His name is Gavin, Gavin the Gorilla. Oh, just one more thing. My real name isn't Mr Nick-Nacks, that's just what I sell on my stall."

"Okay, Mr Normans, I shall remember that. See you next week."

"Well done, Robin. You have bought a gorilla and a little dog for 50 pence; that's quite a good deal! Now, let's have a look and see what we can find for your grandma. After all, she has a birthday coming up," Grandad said.

"What do you think she would like, Grandad?"

"Well, Robin, she is always
complaining about her old
bicycle. The other day she

complained that the basket fell off, then she got a puncture ... and the paint is peeling. But it's hardly surprising; it's one of those antique bicycles, and she has had it since we got married."

"Oh really? And how long is that, Grandad?"

"Oh, I can't remember, Robin. It seems like hundreds of years."

They wandered around and around, and it was by sheer luck

that Grandad found what he was looking for. With their missions accomplished, they jumped back into Grandad's little red car and made their way to his house.

Robin burst through the door with his usual enthusiasm, and Grandma was waiting for him in the kitchen.

"Hello, Grandma! What smells so nice?"

"Good morning, dear. I've baked you boys an extra special vanilla sponge cake to have with your tea."

"Oh, thank you, Grandma," said Robin.

"Thank you for the cake, Mabel, it looks lovely," remarked Grandad. "I have bought you something rather special from the car boot sale."

"Oh really, Harry? What is it?" Grandma looked a little suspicious.

"Well, you know how you are always complaining about your old bicycle?"

"Yes, Harry, it keeps falling to bits and getting punctures. But what do you expect? I have had it since we were married; it's practically an antique."

"Here is your present, dear, and it's brand new."

Grandad handed her the present.

"Oh, Harry! How generous of you. Are you sure you can afford it?"

"Mabel, when it's for you, I don't care how much I spend."

"Yes, Harry, I can see that!"

"It's an antique bicycle puncture repair kit! They're not easy to come by, you know, not for bicycles as old as that one. In fact, to tell you the truth, it cost nearly as much as a brand new bicycle!"

Grandma looked angry.

"Harry, I really wonder about you sometimes," she said as she walked off.

When Grandma had gone, Grandad cut two slices of cake and Robin put the toys on the kitchen table. Then Grandad said his magic spell...

"Little toy, hear this rhyme,
Let it take you back in time,
Tales of sadness or of glory,
Little toy, reveal your story."

The toy gorilla began to shake a little; then he blinked the way that gorillas do when they wake up in strong sunlight.

He seemed frightened and looked around for somewhere to hide.

"Don't be frightened, we are not going to hurt you!" Robin said.

"Who are you?" the gorilla asked.

"Well, I am Robin and this is my grandad."

"Where is Snuffles? I want Snuffles."

"It's alright, he is still in the bag. He hasn't woken up yet."

Suddenly, there was loud barking, followed by a growling, snarling sound.

"It's alright, Snuffles," said the gorilla. "They are very friendly; they are not going to hurt us. Calm down, Snuffles."

"Don't worry," said Robin.

"Grandad and I woke you up.

We know that you are called

Gavin and that the little dog

is called Snuffles, but we don't know much about gorillas. Will you please tell us about them?"

"*Well yes, I would love to. Please make yourselves comfortable and I shall begin...*

"Gorillas are the largest of the primates, and most people believe that we are distant relatives of man. There are two main types of gorilla."

He spun around and pointed to his back.

"You see, I have a black back, and my cousins have silver backs. So I am called a Black Back gorilla and they are called Silver Back gorillas."

"Yes, that makes sense, but where is your home?"

"Well, we originated in the forests of central Africa, although some of us live in high areas and are called Mountain gorillas."

"You all look so big and strong and scary. Are you dangerous?"

"*No, Robin, don't be fooled by all that shouting and chest thumping. If we are left alone to get on with our lives, we are quite happy. We just like peace and quiet.*"

"Okay, that sounds fine, but do you eat people?"

Gavin laughed.

"No, of course not, don't be silly!

We eat mainly fruit and vegetables; you know, bananas, leaves, that sort of stuff. We are what scientists call herbivores."

"Wow! That's fascinating, thank you. But how did you and Snuffles come to be on the car boot sale stall?"

"Oh, that's a long story. Do you have the time to listen to it?"

"Oh yes, of course, please tell us."

" Well, as you may know, gorillas are quite rare. That means there are not many of us left in the wild, and some men

are horrid to us. So our
government   thought   that   we
would be safer in a safari park.

     "So that's where I ended
up. I grew up amongst lots of
different animals and a few
humans. I remember once,
when I was little, I was trying
to climb a tree, imitating some
spider monkeys, when I fell
and landed on my head.

"I took quite a knock, and my mum was very worried because I was bleeding. She didn't know what to do, but fortunately, one of the keepers saw me and took me to see this special type of human called a vet.

"I didn't know what a vet was and I was a bit scared, but the vet was very nice to me. She gave me some medicine to stop my head hurting and fixed the cut on my head. Then she sent me back to my mum.

"After that day I saw the vet heal lots of animals, and I realised that was going to be my mission in life. I really wanted to be a vet too so that I could help nurse injured animals back to health.

"While I was young there wasn't too much of a problem. Animals would let me hang around and try to help them; they just thought I was a curious kid. But as I grew up, they started to run away from me. I only wanted to help them,

but they avoided me like I was

some big, scary monster.

"Then, one night, I saw a little lost antelope looking for his mum. He looked really frightened. I tried to go up to him to help him find her, but he must have thought I wanted to hurt him. He ran away from me so quickly that he tripped and hurt his leg.

"When the other animals found out, they all came after me. They thought that I'd tried to hurt the poor baby antelope! But I just wanted to help! I was devastated.

"I realised that although I only wanted to help, no one would ever trust a big, scary-looking gorilla like me. So I thought it was best for me to leave; that way, the other animals wouldn't have to be afraid of me any more.

"I knew that stray gorillas didn't have too many job options, so I was fortunate to be able to join a passing circus.

"Circus life was alright,
and everything was going well.
I even learned to juggle
bananas!

"Unfortunately, it all ended on a bad note when one night I got hungry and ate the props.

"After that I wandered the streets trying to find somewhere to live. After knocking on a few doors, I realised that gorillas aren't generally made welcome in middle-class homes.

"So I headed away from civilisation and ended up living all alone in a cave.

"It was getting late one evening when I heard a terrible crashing sound; it came from the nearby road, so I went to see what had happened.

"There had been a car crash. All the car doors had jammed shut and there was a family still inside. I tried to open the doors to get them out, but they were locked tight.

"I used all of my strength, and managed to break off the doors and get the people out.

"They were alright, but very scared of me, so I ran away back to my cave to hide.

"Then I heard a yap, yap, yap. A little dog had followed me.

"I wasn't sure what he wanted. I was used to people running away from me; no one had ever followed me before!

"The little dog introduced himself and told me his name was Snuffles. He thanked me for saving him, and he even licked my hand! I couldn't believe it! He didn't think I was going to hurt him or eat him. He was one of the smallest, most fragile animals I'd ever seen, but he wasn't scared of me at all.

"Snuffles decided to stay with me, and we became very good friends.

"I asked him how a little dog like him had become so brave, and he told me that he had ten brothers and sisters. He was born last, and was the smallest and weakest, and he always had to fight hard to get his meals.

"As he got older, his brothers and sisters picked on him a lot, but Snuffles learned to fight back and earned their respect.

"Snuffles felt a bit sorry for me because he realised that, despite my size and scary appearance, I was just a big softy, a real gentle giant, but that's what he really liked about me.

"Snuffles, on the other hand, despite his cuddly appearance, wasn't scared of anything or anyone. We were complete opposites.

"We were the best of friends living in our little cave, but it didn't last long. One morning, I went out to get the newspaper and suddenly felt a sharp pain in my arm ... and that's all I remember.

"I woke up somewhere strange with quite a headache,

and a little dog was licking my face. 'Snuffles,' I said, 'what has happened?'

" 'Well, Gavin,' he growled, 'it would seem that when you saved me and the people in the car, they reported to the police that they had seen a gorilla and were very frightened of it. So the police contacted the local safari park, who sent some men to capture you.

" 'They used a tranquiliser dart to knock you out and then brought you back to the safari park.

" 'Although you had passed out, I wasn't going to let anyone within an inch of you. I put up quite a fight. I guess they must have realised we were friends, because they brought me here too.'

"I really wasn't happy to be back at the safari park. I knew how much all the other animals hated me and I tried to avoid them, but at least I had Snuffles for company!

"I had done really well to stay out of trouble, until one night I was awoken by the sound of crying. I got up and followed the crying to the lake, and there, splashing around for dear life, was a little baby gazelle. I jumped in and swam over to rescue her, but she was obviously very scared and put up quite a struggle.

"I managed to get her to dry land, where she curled up in my arms, and we both fell asleep under a tree.

"When I woke up the next morning, I was surrounded by angry animals. The lion roared at me, and said that because the baby gazelle was alright they wouldn't hurt me, but he told me to pack my bananas and leave.

"At that moment, Snuffles stormed over and gave them a good telling off. He told them how I had saved the baby gazelle from drowning and that they should be ashamed for always thinking the worst about me, just because I was big and scary looking.

"After that I went about my life as usual, until one day I had a strange surprise when the baby gazelle's mum came to see me. She said she had to go and visit her sister, and asked me if I could babysit the baby gazelle. I was delighted; I couldn't believe that she would trust me with such a big responsibility.

"I looked after the baby gazelle all day, and before I knew it, lots of the mums from the safari park wanted me to *babysit their young ones too.*

"I eventually became so popular that Snuffles and I opened a day care centre in the safari park. All my life I had wanted to look after other animals, and thanks to Snuffles, my dream came true!"

"Wow, Gavin, that's a lovely story!" said Robin. "You were so lucky that your friend saw how good you really were and helped everyone else see it too."

"*I certainly was,*" said Gavin, "*and a lot of people could learn from my story.*"

Robin already had.

On Monday morning, the first lesson was games, and it was the start of the cricket season. Mr Jolly, the Games Teacher, came bouncing into class.

"Alright, class, everybody follow me into the gym."

Once they got to the gym, they were all lined up.

"Right, everybody!" shouted Mr Jolly.

He always shouted; Robin assumed that shouting must be a necessary qualification for a games teacher.

"The cricket season has started and I want two of you to pick ten other players. Robin, you're captain of A team. Who do you want to pick first?"

Robin didn't have to think twice.

"I shall pick Mark."

Everybody sniggered.

There was still some pointing and laughing going on when they had finished picking the teams, and there was quite a lot more laughing when Robin sent Mark out to bat first.

But when Mark hit the cricket ball out of the playing field, he was met with stunned silence...

"Six!" shouted a wobbly voice in the background.

Another boy shouted, 'Lucky!" But it wasn't luck. Mark hit every ball over the boundary.

Suddenly, everybody forgot what they had thought about him in the past, and there certainly wasn't any laughing when he was made captain of the school's cricket team.